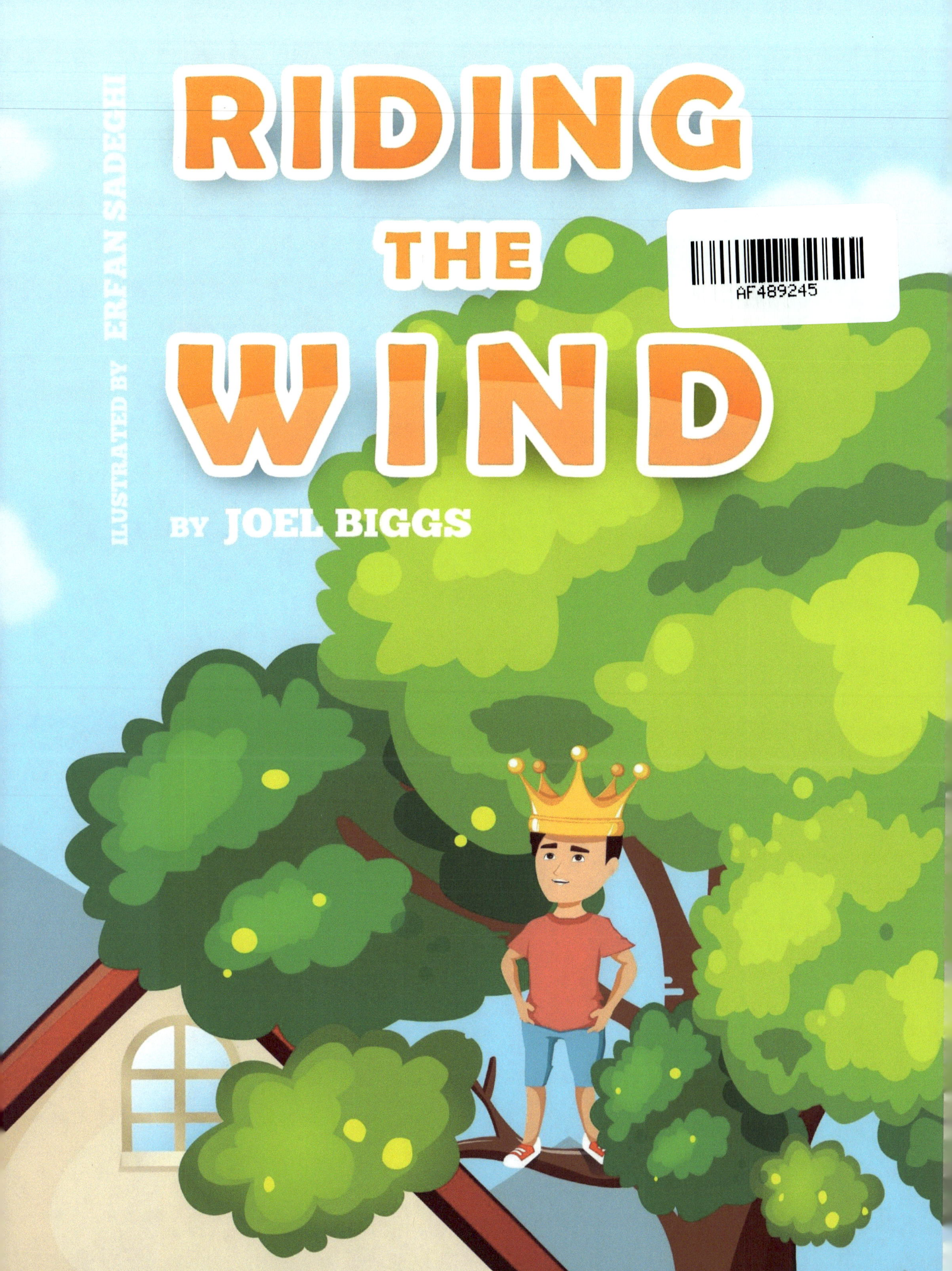

RIDING THE WIND
ILLUSTRATED BY ERFAN SADEGHI
BY JOEL BIGGS
AF489245

In the front corner of the yard, sitting all by itself, was this massive oak tree.

It was taller than any tree on our tree on our street and it towered majestically over every house in our neighborhood and it belonged to me.

In it's arms I could climb mountains, sail pirate ships, see on-coming armies, or ride the wind like Superman.

It was my hiding place, where every-
one was the size of ants and I was
their king.

Sometimes they would see me and smile, remembering their times in a tree.

Brown and gray branches reached as if trying to touch the sea of turquoise in the not so distant sky.

The dark green leaves with
their light green bellies, of
the big old oak tree,
clapped with one another,
like an excited crowd.

As the ancient giant swayed
and bounced, in a wind
that came from
everywhere

I held on even though it
felt like an old friend was
holding on to me.

I would always inch my way towards
the top, as it rocked back and forth,
like grandma's rocking chair.

The wind ruffled my hair without any purpose, first in my eyes then out, then in my mouth and out.

Then it would tickle my ears, always swirling in all directions as the peak came closer and closer.

The blue reached for me, toyed with me, urging me to reach higher and higher.

The clouds, huge patches of cotton candy, raced by, like they were late for a fair.

One looked like a horse, streching for the finish line.

Another one looked like my aunt Martha, with her nose wrinkled and twisted.

It was like the face she makes when she smells something funny.

Another one looked like our neighbor's cat when she screeched, with her hair standing up when my dog Butch ran after her.

Most of them looked like faces in a crowd of people who were waiting for a bus, some bored, some talking, some were even smiling.

The branches would lean and bend
to the dancing of the wind.

Instead of being bucked off, like a cowboy on a horse in the rodeo.

I would ride with my tree like waves on the ocean, on the branches of my friend.

The wind would sometimes whip and blow, grab and pull.

But my old friend would hold onto me with it's weathered grasp, that felt like grandpa's leathery calloused hands.

Up at the top, the faint smell of bacon would linger for a moment from someone's breakfast.

But in a flash it would be gone, only to be replaced by the most comfortable smell in the world, the smell of cut grass.

The comfort it brings swirls in my nose and is gone, and then it's back again, teasing me.

Trying to get me to
lean further out to it,
but still my old friend
holds me on.

When I'm riding the wind, I am with heros or heading to our next adventure.

Not worrying about homework or chores, or fighting with my brothers, or upset that I was picked last.

Everything was
right with the
world, between
my old friend
and me.

I'm was on top of the world, I was the king, and it was my country...

www.ingramcontent.com/pod-product-compliance
Lightning Source LLC
Chambersburg PA
CBHW042014110726
48006CB00004B/1077